This is an adventure story based on the game of chess. The text is in two parts, each aimed at a different age group and level of interest in the game.

The main story is for complete beginners and attempts to convey the basic rules and ideas of chess in an unobtrusive fashion, as part of the narrative.

The story is supported by short, self-contained captions, each one dealing with some fundamental rule or approach in more detail.

The two levels have been written to complement each other: the story to amuse and stimulate, the captions to provide more information.

The whole effort is intended, like the game itself, to be a lot of fun. Enjoy it!

YOUR MOVE

MICHAEL FITZPATRICK
Illustrated by Andy Kelly

THE O'BRIEN PRESS • DUBLIN

First published 1990 by The O'Brien Press Ltd.
20 Victoria Road, Rathgar, Dublin 6, Ireland.

British Library Cataloguing in Publication Data
Fitzpatrick, Michael
Your move: a chess adventure for young beginners.
1. Chess
I. Title
794.1

ISBN 0-86278-196-5

10 9 8 7 6 5 4 3 2 1

Typesetting and layout: The O'Brien Press
Printed by Colour Books, Dublin, Ireland

The O'Brien Press receives assistance from
The Arts Council / An Comhairle Ealaíon.

Once upon a time,
in the Kingdom
of the Sixty-four
Squares . . .

. . . the White King turned to the queen and said, 'Bah!'

'Yes, dear,' said the White Queen, wondering what exactly the king was going to complain about this time. She didn't have to wonder for very long.

'I'm fed up,' the king announced. 'Fed up sharing this kingdom with that grumpy old Black King and his gang. I think I'll call my advisors and army together and go out and beat him once and for all.'

The White Queen was delighted. 'Yes, dear,' she said, 'that sounds like a very good idea. It gets so boring not being able to go just where one pleases. Constantly bumping into those wretched people and being forced to stay in our own part of the kingdom. One good battle and you'd be in complete control.'

THE BOARD

Every chess board has 64 squares – 32 white and 32 black.

Put your board flat on a table and look at the right-hand corner nearest to you. What colour is the square at the right-hand corner? If it is a black square, turn the board around until you have a white square at the right-hand corner.

The board is now ready for you to put the pieces out. Always remember to check this right-hand corner before you begin – you should always have white on your right.

The White King said nothing for a while. He was thinking. When he finally spoke, he had a worried frown on his face.

'I have very good advisors . . . my knights are the best in the land . . . my castles are strong . . . my soldiers fearless . . .'

'So, what's the trouble, dear?' the queen asked.

'Well, it's just that the Black army seems to be fairly well organised too. It's not as simple as just going out there and knocking the stuffing out of them. THEY might beat US.'

That started the queen thinking. 'I see what you mean,' she said. 'But surely we can come up with a plan that will help us to defeat the Black forces, some trick that will lure them to their doom? I know just who can help us to cook up such a devilish scheme – send for the bishops.'

The two White Bishops were summoned into the royal presence. They sidled in and took their places beside the two monarchs, the Queen's Bishop by her side, the King's Bishop by his. Tall, imposing figures in their pointy hats, they both had a habit of looking at things at an angle. There was nothing straightforward about the two bishops! The king explained that he wanted them to come up with a plan that would overcome the Black forces.

'And be quick about it,' he added.

The bishops glanced sideways at each other and started thinking. The King's Bishop was the first to speak.

'Attacking the Black King and taking control is a very good idea,' he said in a squeaky voice, 'but I really don't think that we bishops should get involved. Not our sort of business, you see.'

The Queen's Bishop nodded in agreement. 'Yes,' he agreed, in an even squeakier voice, 'this is a job for knights, castles and those little pawn chaps.'

'Anyway,' said the King's Bishop, 'whatever you decide to do will depend on what the Black King's forces do when you do something to them . . . if you see what I mean.'

WHAT GOES WHERE?

Count the pieces in your chess set. Unless the dog has swallowed a few of them, you should have 32 pieces altogether, 16 white and 16 black. We can now place them in their proper starting positions on the board. First, we place one white castle on the white right-hand corner square. Next, we place a white knight beside the castle. Then comes the first white bishop, then the white king, then the white queen. Moving away from the queen, we copy the other side of the board exactly, bishop first, then knight, with the other white castle last, out on the black square at the left corner of the board.

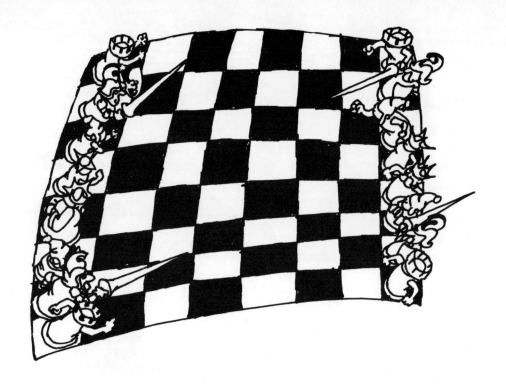

AND THE SAME FOR BLACK

Having seen how we position the white pieces at one end of the board, you should now have very little trouble placing the black pieces at the other end. Just remember that the black pieces must be in exactly the same positions as the white ones, but at the other side of the board.

There is just one small difficulty with the positions and that is where to put the king and queen. When you have all the other pieces in position, there are two squares left free in the middle of the back row.

Which one is for the king and which one for the queen? Does it matter? Well, yes, it matters a great deal. The white queen must be on a white square at the start, and the black queen must be on a black square. That means that the two kings go onto the only two remaining spaces. The simplest way to remember this is always to place your queen on her own colour — if you have white, your queen must start on white; if you have black, your queen must start on black.

The king clearly didn't. He stared down at the black and white floor in silence for a few minutes. Finally the queen spoke. 'Perhaps you should send for your knights, dear?'

The two knights came clattering in and took their places beside the bishops, the King's Knight beside the King's Bishop, the Queen's Knight beside the Queen's Bishop – a very orderly place, the Kingdom of the Sixty-Four Squares! The queen thought that the two knights looked rather strange, a little horsey in fact, but she was too polite to say anything. Then the White King spoke.

'Good knights . . .' he began.

'Good night, Your Highness,' they answered together.

'Thank you,' said the king,

getting
very
confused
since it
was only
ten o'clock in the
morning. 'We are going
to attack the Black army
and take over the whole
kingdom.'

The two knights were delighted.

'Bravo!' said the King's Knight.

'Jolly good!' said the Queen's
Knight.

'I told you so,' said one bishop.

'Just the men for the job,' said
the other.

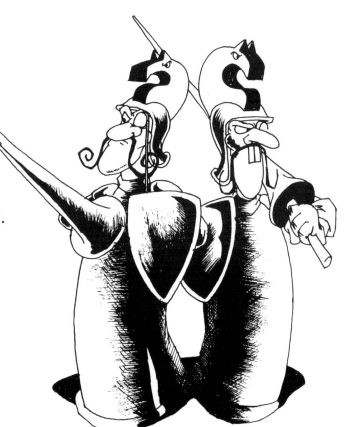

'So what do you recommend?' asked the king.

Suddenly, there was complete silence.

'Well . . .' said the Queen's Knight.

'Em . . .' said the other.

There was more complete silence.

The White Queen knew that it was rude to stare, but she couldn't help looking at the King's Knight as he paced around, gazing at the floor. He was doing the strangest thing. He would move forward two squares and then step sideways. Or sideways two squares and then up one. He never seemed to be where she expected.

How very peculiar, thought the queen. I must mention that to the king. Just then she realised that her own knight was at it too, and was just as bad: two squares across and one up or down, leaping over anything that got in the way.

It must be all that military training, the queen said to herself, adding out loud, 'Gentlemen, we all seem to agree that an attack on the Black army is a good idea, but no one has a clue how to go about it.'

KNIGHT MOVES

The knight is probably the hardest piece to learn how to move because, unlike all the other pieces, it doesn't go in straight lines. The knights are also the only pieces on the board which can jump over other pieces – a trick which will often catch your opponent by surprise. Think of the knight's move as the letter L – one square across and two squares up, or two squares across and one square up, in any direction.

Nobody said anything, so the White Queen continued. 'We are well protected here, with castles at both ends of the kingdom and a line of fighting men between us and the enemy. Why don't we send out one of those pawns from the front line and see what happens?'

The two bishops were delighted that the queen's plan didn't involve them in any risk. The two knights were a little annoyed that they hadn't thought of it first, but both agreed that it wasn't a bad way of starting a fight.

'So,' said the king in a loud voice, looking at the eight pawns standing in line in front of the royal party, 'we'll be needing a volunteer.'

PAWN POSITIONS

Having put eight white pieces on the first row of the board, we still have eight white pieces left over. These are all the same size and shape and are called pawns. The starting position for the pawns is very simple — they stand side-by-side on the second row of the board, just in front of the other white pieces.

Each of the eight soldiers suddenly seemed to be thinking of something else. Nobody moved.

'You!' shouted the king, jabbing the soldier in front of him. 'What's your name?'

'P-P-Peewee Pawn, Sir.'

'This is your lucky day, Peewee,' said the king. 'I have a special job for you.'

'Th-th-thank you, Sir,' said poor old Peeewee, beginning to wish that he hadn't bothered coming in to work.

WHO MOVES FIRST?

White always moves first in the game of chess. To decide which player will get white, one player hides a white pawn in one hand and a black pawn in the other. The other player now chooses a hand. If he chooses the hand with the white pawn, he will play with white and will have the first move. There are many different moves with which you can start the game. Most players begin by moving one of the central pawns – they are the two pawns in front of the king and queen. Let's say you decide to move the king pawn. Now you have a choice: you can move it forward one square, or, if you wish, two squares. Every one of the eight pawns gives you the same choice – either one or two squares forward – but only the first time you move any single pawn. The second time you move any pawn, you have no choice, you can only move it one square forward. Pawns never move backwards.

'I want you to advance and attack the Black army,' announced the White King.

Peewee reeled. 'Y-y-you're too kind, Highness,' he stammered, 'but really, I couldn't. I feel a headache coming on. I'm not the man for the job. And my mother told me not to talk to strangers.'

'You don't have to TALK to them,' cackled the Queen's Bishop, 'just go out and beat them up!'

'I'm s-s-sorry,' mumbled Peewee, 'but the sight of violence makes me ill, especially when I'm likely to be the victim!'

'We'll all be with you,' said the queen, giving Peewee a special smile. 'You have absolutely nothing to fear.'

Peewee began to feel quite brave after that. All be with you – nothing to fear – and the queen had such a nice face!

22

When the king ordered 'Forward, march', Peewee shot out two squares to the middle of the kingdom without as much as a thought.

Then he saw another face, and it wasn't as nice as the queen's! The whole Black army was now watching him, but Peewee looked straight ahead, right into the mean, piggy eyes of the most enormous Black Pawn he had ever seen. Before Peewee had a chance to realise how terrified he was, things got worse. Much worse.

24

At an order from the Black King, the mountain with mean eyes advanced from the Black ranks and stopped right in front of Peewee. Peewee closed his eyes, expecting the worst. Nothing happened.

When nothing had happened for a while longer, Peewee opened his eyes again. The Black Pawn had his eyes closed too, and he appeared to be praying. He didn't look half as big or as vicious as Peewee had thought. In fact, he was exactly the same size as Peewee. When he finally opened his eyes, they were staring at each other, almost nose to nose.

'Hello,' said Peewee, who felt it would be rude to ignore the Black Pawn, besides being very difficult.

'I beg your pardon?' said the Black Pawn in a startled voice. 'I really don't think I should talk to you. We haven't been introduced. And besides, you're the enemy.'

'Oh,' said Peewee, confused. 'So, what are you going to do next?'

'To tell you the truth,' said the Black Pawn, 'I don't really know. I can't go any further with you in the way. And I can't do anything to get you out of the way.'

'Really?' Peewee said, becoming more confused by the minute.

'Don't you know anything about being a pawn?' asked the Black soldier.

'Not a lot,' admitted Peewee. 'I've led a sheltered life so far. This is all rather new to me.'

The other pawn seemed to relax a bit. 'In that case, stick around, kid. You've got a lot to learn!'

Peewee couldn't really argue with that, so he said nothing. He decided to have a look around and see what was happening. There didn't seem to be very much going on in either army, just a lot of mumbling and pointing.

'It'll take them a while to decide what to do next,' said the Black Pawn, 'so I'll just fill you in on a few of the basics. The first thing to remember is that this is a battle. The White army is going to try to capture the Black King; the Black army will try to stop them and see if they can capture the White King. Do you follow?'

Peewee wasn't sure that he did, but he just nodded and tried to look knowledgeable.

'Good,' said the Black Pawn. 'The second thing to remember is that the life of a pawn is not as simple as it seems. Even if we don't have all the fancy moves of the bigger pieces, we're still very important. Pawns move straight ahead, but they attack at an angle . . .'

This was too much for Peewee. 'I don't mean to seem stupid,' he said, 'but what's "attack" and how do you mean "angle"?'

The Black Pawn went red in the face and wobbled a bit. 'You really DO have a lot to learn,' he said with a funny smile. 'Okay. Do you see this square to my left?'

Peewee nodded.

'And this square to my right?'

Peewee nodded again.

'Well, if any member of the Black army moves into either one of those squares, you can just move in at an angle and take them.'

'And what does "take" mean?' Peewee asked in a quiet voice, hoping that the Black Pawn would answer the question without realising he'd even been asked one.

It didn't work. The Black Pawn's eyes bulged and he wobbled in two complete circles before answering through clenched teeth.

'No offence,' the Black Pawn said in a strangled voice, 'but you really are the most complete dope I have ever met! "Taking" is what it's all about! If you land on a square which already has one of the Black army on it, you can take him – he's had it, finished, done with. He's a gonner – no more.'

The Black Pawn was getting quite excited. Peewee was afraid to ask any more questions but, luckily, the Black Pawn was just catching his breath and wasn't finished giving out answers.

'Once you take one of the opposition, he's out of the battle, he can't help his side anymore. He has to watch the rest of the action from the sideline.'

'And is that the worst thing that can happen,' Peewee asked, suddenly excited too, 'just being taken out of the battle?'

The Black Pawn changed colour several times and went for a short wobble.

'What could be worse? Out of the struggle, no chance to be heroic, forced to watch? Terrible!'

Peewee smiled to himself and said nothing.

Just then, the most amazing noise made him turn around. He saw the White King's Knight leap two squares forward over the heads of the startled pawns still in line. The knight then skidded one square sideways, to come to rest just behind Peewee, a little to his right.

'There you are, m'boy,' panted the knight. 'Told you I'd be right behind you. Let me just get my breath back and we'll see about sweeping that Black Pawn fellow out of your way.'

Peewee didn't like the sound of that at all, but before he could say anything, things started happening in the Black army. The pawn in front of the Black Queen shuffled forward just one square, so that he was behind Peewee's Black friend, a little to the left.

'Phew,' said Peewee's friend, turning to the new arrival, 'I'm glad you're here.'

'That's Pompous Pawn,' he explained to Peewee, 'the Black Queen's favourite. A bit of a bore to be honest, but he'll keep your knight off my back for a while.'

'I don't understand,' said a bewildered Peewee. 'Why did he move just one square forward? Why didn't he move two squares like we did? And how can he help you against the knight?'

The Black Pawn gave Peewee a hard look and then decided to be patient.

'That's about the only freedom pawns have,' he explained, with just the slightest tremor in his voice. 'On our first move, each of us can advance either one square or two squares. After that, it's a pretty slow business, one step at a time. And we can never turn back.'

'I see,' said Peewee, who had never realised that life could be so complicated. 'Now explain how he's helping you.'

'Well,' said the Black Pawn, 'if your friend the White Knight there wanted to, he could advance two squares and across one in the strange way those knights have, and land right here – on top of me! But after he'd taken me, old Pompous would take him and the Black army would be delighted. We'd only lose a pawn, you'd lose a knight!'

Suddenly, with a curious swishing noise, the White King's Bishop came zooming out to stop in the centre of the kingdom, just one black square away from Peewee.

'Bless you, my child,' said the bishop to Peewee, before fixing the lines of the Black army with a vicious scowl.

'Don't like the look of him,' whispered the Black Pawn to Peewee, 'but he's not my worry at the moment.'

'What do you mean?'

'Look where he's standing.'

Peewee did, and saw nothing.

'He's standing on a white square,' explained the Black Pawn. 'That's the way he moves all through the game, diagonally along the white squares. As long as I stay on a black square, he can't get me. It's your other bishop, the one who moves along the black diagonals, that I have to worry about.'

BISHOPS – A MIXED BLESSING

The bishops are tricky characters. They always move in straight lines, but they move diagonally. That simply means that they travel at an angle to the sides of the board, always staying on squares of the same colour. You will see that one of your bishops is standing on a white square and one is standing on black. They will both stay on the same colour all through the game because of their forward-and-sideways diagonal move. Like the castles and the queen, bishops can move any number of squares, provided there are no other pieces in the way.

Peewee would like to have asked what 'diagonally' meant, but he never had a chance. More things were happening in the Black ranks. Peewee couldn't see what was going on very clearly, but the Black army was obviously excited about something. The two Black bishops were talking, the knights were talking, the king was talking – all very loudly, and all at the same time.

Suddenly, the Black Queen hissed 'Silence!' and everyone shut up. Then, with a regal smile, she swooped diagonally out to the black square just behind Peewee's friend. Peewee nearly died.

'What . . . ?' he began in a whisper, but it was clear that the Black Pawn was no longer listening. He looked as if he had suddenly gone deaf, turned to stone, and been completely paralysed. His eyes glazed over like a dead fish and he looked past Peewee as if Peewee didn't exist.

QUICK-ACTING QUEEN

The queen is the most powerful piece on the board. She can move any number of squares, provided that no other piece blocks her way. She can move in straight lines parallel to the sides of the board, or she can move along the diagonals, just like the bishops. Because she is so powerful, it is not wise to risk losing her in the early stages of the battle and most players will wait until the game has developed before they send out the queen.

'You won't get any information out of him for a while,' said the White Knight behind Peewee. 'Now that their queen has joined the fray, the whole Black army will be on their best behaviour. And we'd better watch out too. Don't be fooled by the good lady's smile. She may look very nice, but she can sweep from one part of the board to another in a flash, and in any direction. Nobody can feel safe when she's around.'

While Peewee was struggling to take in all this new information and trying to make sense of what was going on, he was startled by a further commotion, this time behind him in the White ranks.

'Whatever can be happening now?' he wondered out loud.

The White Knight glanced casually over his shoulder and said, 'Oh that? They're just going to tuck the White King in safely by castling. Happens in nearly every battle. Nothing to get excited about.'

Peewee was amazed by what was going on in the White ranks. Castling, my goodness! he thought.

Because the knight and bishop on the king's side had already left their starting places and were out on the board, there was nothing between the White King and his Castle on the far right-hand corner. First, the king moved two squares to the right – But I thought kings moved only one square at a time? wondered Peewee – and then the King's Castle jumped over the king to land on the King's Bishop's starting position.

Peewee was stunned. 'Surely only knights can jump over other pieces like that? What is going on?'

'It's very simple, really,' said the White Knight in a bored voice. 'Castling is a special move which you can do only once in any battle. And that's the way it's done. The king moves in towards the corner, and the castle comes out to protect him. With the three pawns in front of them, it's a very safe place for the king to be. If we don't look after our king, we might as well pack up and go home, eh?'

Peewee was still looking fairly bemused.

'If you think that's complicated,' said the White Knight, 'just wait until you're in a battle where the king decides to castle on the queen's side of the kingdom. It could take you a week to recover from the shock of that!'

CARING FOR THE KING

Although the queen is the most powerful piece on the board, the king is the most important. He must be looked after at all costs since, once you can no longer protect him, the game is over and you have lost. Since the king moves very slowly – only one square at a time, in any directon, provided there is no other piece in the way – a very good way of protecting the king is called 'castling'. This simply means moving the king onto the square normally occupied by the knight, and then moving the castle onto the bishop's square. All this counts as just one single move. Remember, you can only castle provided there are no pieces between the king and the castle which is going to protect him, provided the king is not already under attack, and provided he does not have to cross a square under attack on his way into the corner.

Peewee had just decided that the knight was joking when he got a REAL shock. Suddenly, a million things seemed to be happening at once. The battle, which had been a rather leisurely affair up until then, finally got down to business and all hell broke loose.

I wish I knew what was happening, thought Peewee. And then things got really confusing.

The Black and White armies seemed to get totally mixed up. A Black Pawn with a funny accent went past Peewee. 'G'day,' he said, 'Platypus Pawn's the name. Catch ya later!'

A lot of other things went past Peewee too. A couple of times, Peewee was just in time to notice members of the Black army staring at him in a funny way. Then he realised they were trying to take him, so he just stepped one square forward, out of the old danger and straight into some new one.

GOING TO WAR

The game of chess is all about attacking your opponent. No matter how you plan a game, you will eventually have to get stuck in and have a go at the opposition forces. The essential thing to remember is that an attack must involve some clear idea of how you will protect your own position while, at the same time, putting pressure on the opposition. If you have no overall plan, you will find it very difficult to win.

THE COMBINED ATTACK

The best way to make an attack work is to use a combination of pieces – not just one bishop or one knight charging off in the direction of the enemy, but several pieces working together to protect one another and give the opponent no real chance of escaping. Remember that it is easy to deal with the threat of one piece on its own. But trying to deal with two or three pieces at the same time is much more tricky. If you make life difficult for your opponent, he has less time to make life difficult for you.

It wasn't too bad after a while though. Peewee began to realise that other members of the White army were protecting him at a distance. If a Black soldier looked like he was going to take Peewee, there always seemed to be a White knight or bishop looking on, ready to take the soldier who was giving Peewee trouble. And so he survived.

Great, he thought, we're all in this together!

By the time the dust settled, the Kingdom of the Sixty-Four Squares was a very different-looking place. Instead of the neat, orderly rows of Black and White soldiers, there were only a few of each army left.

I suppose all the others got taken, Peewee thought. I wonder who's winning?

CHECKING THE OPPOSITION

When a combination works well, your opponent will be left with very few moves and very few places to hide his king. When you manage to attack the king – that is, when you could take him on your next move if your opponent did nothing to pre- vent you – this is called check. The oppo- nent must either move the king out of check, or take the piece which is doing the checking, or put one of his own pieces in the way.

He was now closer to the Black end of the kingdom and could see more clearly what was going on. There didn't seem to be too many Black pieces left. When he looked around, Peewee realised that there weren't too many White survivors either. Still, the White King was smiling happily out from behind his protective wall of pawns, while the Black King was stuck in the middle of the board, looking as if he'd seen better days.

Then Peewee heard somebody shouting. 'Take him, take him, take him quick!' was all he could make out. When he turned around to see what the fuss was about, he realised that HE was what all the fuss was about – the White army was shouting at him!

Peewee decided to be cool, calm and collected. He wasn't going to panic under pressure. No sir! Depend on Peewee Pawn in a tight spot! He knew he could only take enemies if they were standing in the line of squares in front of him, either to the left or the right.

So Peewee looked to the left – nothing.

Then he looked to the right and saw what all the shouting was about. One of the Black Knights was standing there, poised to make his L-shaped move and take either a White Castle or the White Knight that Peewee had been talking to earlier.

Well, we can't have that, said Peewee to himself, calmly stepping across and taking the Black Knight. The cheering from the White army nearly deafened him.

'Good man,' yelled the White King.

'Spiffing work,' said the White Castle.

'Thanks a lot, kid,' said the White Knight.

'Damn, now we're really in trouble,' mumbled the Black King.

Peewee was delighted. But there was even better to come.

'Don't stop now,' was the general yell from the White ranks, so Peewee took one further step forward, right up beside the very worried-looking Black King.

'Check!' cried the White army. 'Double damn,' grumbled the Black King. The Black King now moved away from Peewee, but another White soldier then attacked him and the cry of 'Check' went up again. There just didn't seem to be anywhere for the Black King to hide. Before he could settle down in any new square, a White piece would move up to attack that square and the Black King would be in check again. The Black King began to look as if he was giving up hope of ever getting away.

After a few more desperate efforts by the Black King to escape from the net of White pieces attacking him, he was finally trapped with nowhere to go.

We've got him, thought Peewee and, sure enough, the cry of 'Checkmate' went up from the White ranks. The only surviving White Bishop leaped up and down and did a very undignified victory tango. The celebrations were general and enthusiastic. People kept coming up to Peewee and clapping him on the back. Even the Black King smiled across at him and said, 'Well done.'

CHECKMATE

Checkmate is the end of the game of chess. This means that one side has the other side's king under attack in such a way that he cannot move to a safe square, cannot take the piece that is attacking him, and cannot put one of his own pieces in the way. There is no escape, nothing he can do, the game is over. Checkmate!

What happens next? Peewee was wondering, when the Black King asked the very same question. Everything suddenly got very quiet.

'Well . . .' said the White King, 'we've won the battle and that's that. I suppose you Black chaps will just have to clear off.'

'What?' the Black King was furious. 'You can't throw us out of the kingdom on the basis of just one little battle. We've lived here all our lives. Where would we go? And anyway, what would you do without us?'

Clearly, the White King was thinking. 'I suppose we could always have a return battle, just to give you another chance,' he said.

'Now you're talking!' agreed the Black King, 'and this time, we'll beat you!'

'Bah!' said the White King.

'Here we go again,' said Peewee . . .

. . . AND THEY FOUGHT HAPPILY EVER AFTER.

HOW TO PLAY CHESS

The OBJECT of chess is to force your opponent's king into a position in which it cannot avoid being captured.

The game is played on the same BOARD as draughts. This has 64 squares – 32 white alternating with 32 black – arranged in RANKS (left to right) and FILES (up and down). Lines of the same colour crossing the board are called DIAGONALS.

Each player has 16 PIECES, different only in colour. There is one king, one queen, two bishops, two knights, two rooks and eight pawns in each set.

The KING moves one square at a time in any direction.

The QUEEN moves any number of squares in a straight line in any direction.

The BISHOP moves any number of squares along the diagonals.

The KNIGHT moves in an L-shape, one square across and two up, or two across and one up, jumping over any piece in the way.

The ROOK moves any number of squares along lines parallel to the sides of the board.

The PAWNS move forward only, one square at a time, except on the first move of each pawn when it may be advanced two squares.

All pieces TAKE and CAPTURE by moving onto the square occupied by an enemy piece. That piece is then removed from the board.

Pawns take by moving at an angle into the next line, to the square either left or right of the one straight in front.

If a pawn reaches the last rank of the enemy side of the board, it may be exchanged for any other piece except the king. This is called PROMOTION. The pawn can become a piece which is still on the board, so that you can have, say, two or more queens, three bishops and so on.

CASTLING is a protective move involving the king and one rook (also called 'castle'). The king moves two squares towards the rook, which is then placed on the square passed over by the king. Castling can be done only once in any game, but to either side of the board. For castling to be permissible there must be no piece between king and rook; neither piece can have been moved earlier in the game; the king must not be in check; and neither the square crossed nor the one moved into by the king can be under attack.

EN PASSANT (a French phrase which means 'in passing') is another strange move involving the pawns. If a pawn is moved two squares forward to land beside an opposing pawn which could have captured it if it had been moved only one square, then the opponent may take the pawn, moving his own piece into the square crossed by the taken piece on its two-square advance. The en passant capture must be done immediately, not as a later move.

When you attack the opposition king, this is known as CHECK. The opponent must either move his king out of check, capture the attacking piece, or move a piece between king and attacker.

When the king can no longer be saved, he is in CHECKMATE (from the Persian words *shah* 'king' and *mat* 'dead') and the game is over. You never take the opposing king – the game ends once he is trapped.